Just Right Family

An Adoption Story

Silvia Lopez   illustrated by Ziyue Chen

Albert Whitman & Company
Chicago, Illinois

For my husband, Orlando, ever patient,
and for all those families willing to look
in their hearts and see a child—SL

To my family and dearest friend, Li Juan—ZC

Library of Congress Cataloging-in-Publication data is on file with the publisher.

Text copyright © 2018 by Silvia Lopez
Illustrations copyright © 2018 by Ziyue Chen
First published in the United States of America in 2018 by Albert Whitman & Company
ISBN 978-0-8075-4082-4 (hardcover)
ISBN 978-0-8075-4083-1 (ebook)

Printed in the United States of America
10 9 8 7 6 5 4 3 JOS 26 25 24 23 22 21

For more information about Albert Whitman & Company,
visit our website at www.albertwhitman.com.

My family is Mama, Papa,
and me, and it's just right.

On Saturdays, Mama starts me off on the park swings.
"Feet back, Meili!" she calls out. "Then up, up!"
My toes reach for the sky. I'm flying!

We feed the ducks. I like the ducks, but the big geese are scary.
"They won't hurt you," Papa says. "I'm here."

We pick out library books.
We read them together.
Mama, Papa, and me.

"Tell me my favorite story," I say every night. It's not in a book. Mama points to the big map on my wall, to a place called China.

"We flew far across the sea to adopt you," she says.

"Why?" I ask.

"We learned you needed a new home," Papa answers. "So we asked to be your forever family."

"We looked in our hearts and saw you there," Mama says. "You were just right."

It's the best story!

My story.

One night, Mama says,
"We have a surprise."
"A puppy?" I ask.
"No, someday a puppy,"
she says. "This is better."

"A sister, Meili," Papa says. "We're going to adopt a baby. Our family is going to grow."

Mama is wrong.

A puppy would be better.

The next morning at breakfast I ask, "Why do we need a baby?
Our family is just right."
"Papa and I looked in our hearts," Mama says, "and saw her there."
Sometimes I wish Mama and Papa didn't do so much looking.

"Will the baby look like me? Or you?" I ask.
"She won't look like any of us, Meili," Mama
answers. "She'll be just right."

"Why doesn't she stay where she is?" I ask Papa on the way to school.

"Sometimes babies need new homes," he says. "We asked to be her forever family. Now Mama and I are double-lucky. We'll have you *and* her!"

He smiles big and hugs me tight.
I hug him back, but I don't smile much.
Me and a puppy would have been lucky enough.

"How do you feel about being a big sister?" my teacher asks.

"I don't know," I say. "I've never been one."

"I think you'll be awesome!" she says. "You're very, very special."

FRID

I'm glad she thinks I'm special.

I smile, just a little.

"Where is the baby now?" I ask.

"In a place called Haiti," Mama says.

On my map, Haiti looks far away.

"Papa and I need to go get her," Mama tells me.

"You're leaving me?" I grumble.

"Only for a week," she says. "Grandma will come stay with you. She has big plans."

When Grandma calls I sing her the new song I learned at school.

She asks about the baby.

"She's coming, I guess," I say. "I got new shoes."

"Then we'll buy a dress to match!" Grandma says. "Got lots of great stuff planned for us to do, kiddo!"

I smile a little bigger.

Mama lets me pick a color for the baby's room.

My room is blue, my favorite. I tell her the baby's room can be pink.

Papa buys a map like mine and hangs it on the wall.

He puts a shiny star sticker on Haiti. Another on China.

And then he puts one where our house is.

"What about my map?" I ask.

Papa opens his hand. Another sticker!

We put a star on Haiti on my map too.

I walk around both rooms.

Blue is still my favorite color.

But I think pink is now my second favorite.

Before they leave, Mama and Papa hold me tight.
"We'll be back before you know it," they say.
I hug Mama hard.

My shirt smells like her perfume the whole day.

One afternoon Grandma and I go see a movie.

It's about a family. I think about Mama and Papa.

I miss them a lot.

"Are they coming back today?" I ask Grandma.

"Not today, Meili. But time will fly, you'll see," she says.

The next day I try on lots of dresses at the mall. Grandma buys me two!

"They both match your new shoes!" she says.

I see a tiny, printed dress. It's pink, like the baby's room. "Can we buy this one too?" I ask. "For the baby?"

Grandma smiles. "Sure."

"When are Mama and Papa coming home?" I ask again.

"Be patient," she says. "It's been almost a week."

Then one morning she says, "Let's go, Meili!"

At the airport Grandma pats my knee as we wait. "Soon..." she says.

Finally I see Papa. And Mama holding a baby.

"I'm so happy!" Grandma whispers. She starts to cry!

Sometimes Grandma's hard to figure out.

"Come meet Sophie, Meili," Papa says.

Sophie takes my finger
and won't let go.

"Hi, Sophie," I tell her. "I'm your sister.

I'm going to help push you on the swings.

I'm going to help keep the geese away.

Do you like stories?"

She gives me a tiny smile.

I smile back big.

That night we read library books together.

Then I tell her a story.

Her story.

I point to the map, to the star on the place called Haiti.

I tell her how Mama and Papa flew over the sea to an island to adopt her.

How we all looked in our hearts and saw her there.

And how we knew she was just right.

Like our family.